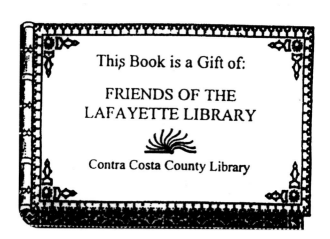

Lizzie and the Last Day of School

Annie   Mae   Ella   Elaine   James   Lizzie

Written by

TRINKA HAKES NOBLE

♥

Illustrated by

KRIS ARO McLEOD

For Ruby and Ivy, who love to learn.
With love,

T.H.N.

For Mom, my friend and mentor
Thank you for everything.

K.A.M.

Text Copyright © 2015 Trinka Hakes Noble
Illustration Copyright © 2015 Kris Aro McLeod

Sleeping Bear Press
315 E. Eisenhower Parkway, Suite 200
Ann Arbor, MI 48108
www.sleepingbearpress.com

Printed and bound in the United States.

10 9 8 7 6 5 4 3 2 1

Noble, Trinka Hakes.
Lizzie and the last day of school / written by Trinka Hakes Noble ;
illustrated by Kris Aro McLeod.
pages cm
Summary: "Lizzie loves school more than anything. After starting first grade, she
mistakenly thinks it will last a full year and is dismayed when it ends in June. Luckily
her first grade teacher applies to teach summer school"— Provided by publisher.
ISBN 978-1-58536-895-2
[1. Schools—Fiction.] I. McLeod, Kris Aro, illustrator. II. Title.
PZ7.N6715Li 2015
[E]—dc23
2014026954

Lizzie loved school.

First she loved nursery school.

Then Lizzie loved kindergarten even more.

She loved the smell of new books and her little desk. She loved hearing the happy voices at playtime. She loved seeing the bright artwork in the halls, and the cool water from the drinking fountain always tasted the best.

In fact, Lizzie loved everything about school!

But when the last day of kindergarten came, Lizzie was sad.

So that summer Lizzie played school with her baby sister, Lulu.

Now Lizzie was going to be a big first grader!

"Your first year of school!" said Mom,
proudly handing her a new pencil case.

"Your first year of school!" said Dad,
proudly handing her a new backpack.

Even baby Lulu gave her a new giant box of crayons.

Yippee! thought Lizzie, *a whole year of school!*

On the first day of school Lizzie's teacher printed her name on the board in big letters.

"But you can call me Miss G.," she smiled. "This is my first year of teaching, and you are my first class! Let's make this the best year of school ever!"

Yippee! thought Lizzie. *Even Miss G. said it was a whole year of school!*

Look how many books we can read!

That fall the librarian, Mrs. Reed, gave them the Centipede Reading Award because they read 100 books. Everyone called them Miss G.'s Little Reading Centipedes.

Lizzie brought home lots of books for Lulu.

That winter Mr. Mussel, the gym teacher, taught them how
to *Hop*, *Skip*, and *Jump* to fast music. Even Miss G. joined in.

"Jump back, everyone!" laughed Mr. Mussel. "Here come Miss G.'s
Jolly Little Jumpers!"

At home, Lizzie showed Lulu how
to *Hop*, *Skip*, and *Jump*!

That spring they won the Nature Study Award for their bee and butterfly garden.

"And the winner is Miss G.'s Honeybees!" announced Mr. Gardner, the science teacher.

Miss G. made them wings, so they buzzed down the hall to their room.

At home, Lizzie let Lulu try on her wings.

Even the cafeteria ladies thought Miss G.'s class was the best because her students ate their peas before their desserts.

"Here come Miss G.'s Little Green Peas!" they cooed.

So Miss G. made them all little green leaf hats to wear at lunchtime to remind them to eat their veggies first.

Lizzie let Lulu wear her leaf hat at dinner.

But one day they didn't go to the library because Mrs. Reed was taking inventory.

Then Miss G. collected all their reading books, but didn't hand out any new ones.

The next day they cleaned out their garden and Mr. Mussel took everyone outside for Field Day.

"But shouldn't we be doing math right now?" asked Lizzie.

Then it happened!

"Class, tomorrow is our last day of school," announced Miss G. "It will be a half day, and we will be cleaning out our desks, so please bring a big bag or box."

All the kids cheered. "Yippee!" they shouted. "Tomorrow is the last day of school!"

But Lizzie didn't cheer. Lizzie didn't shout yippee.
Lizzie just frowned.

That night Lizzie was very sad.

"Tomorrow is the last day of school," she cried.
"Not even a whole day, just a half!"

"Look," said Mom, trying to cheer her up, "baby Lulu is bringing you chalk. She wants you to write the ABCs for her."

But Lizzie was too sad to play school with baby Lulu.

The next morning Lizzie's school was bursting with happy noise. In no time, everyone's desks were cleaned out. Everyone hugged and waved good-bye. Everyone ran out the door... everyone except Lizzie.

Lizzie was the last one to leave. She didn't even hug Miss G. good-bye!

But halfway home, Lizzie stopped. "This can't be the last day," she demanded. "It was supposed to be a whole year of school!"

So Lizzie sneaked back, just to make sure. Besides, she wanted to give Miss G. a hug.

School papers littered the sidewalk and parking lot. But Mr. Broom, the janitor, was stretched out in a lounge chair, sipping lemonade.

"Mr. Broom, shouldn't you be sweeping up these papers?" Lizzie asked.

"Hey, kid, school's out for summer. I'm taking the afternoon off!"

Lizzie slipped in the back door. Loud music was booming from the teachers' lounge. Lizzie looked in.

The teachers were partying!!

But Miss G. wasn't there, so Lizzie tiptoed down the hall toward her room.

The hall seemed too long, too quiet, and too empty. No kids lined up at the drinking fountain, no brightly colored artwork on the walls, no shiny planets and stars hanging from the ceiling. Lizzie felt very sad and lonely.

Lizzie peeked in and saw Miss G., who looked just as sad and lonely as Lizzie.

"Miss G.," whispered Lizzie softly, "I came back to give you a hug."

As the two hugged, Miss G. sighed, "Oh, Lizzie, you're just like me!
We both love school so much that the last day makes us sad!"

Being just like Miss G. made Lizzie feel better!

Just then, the school secretary came running in, waving an envelope.

"Miss G.! Miss G.! You got a special delivery from the Town Parks Department!"

Miss G. opened the letter. "Yippee!" she exclaimed. "I'm going to teach summer school in the Town Park! And Lizzie, you can come! No last day of school for you or me!"

Now it was Lizzie's turn to yell *Yippee!*

As the two walked down the hall, hand in hand,
Miss G. told Lizzie all about summer school.

"We'll make a kite and learn how to fly it!" she said excitedly. "Oh, there'll be swimming lessons twice a week! We'll take nature walks to study bugs and frogs, and a trip to a farm to learn about tomatoes and watermelons... And of course, we'll have story time and snacks every day under the big shade tree..."

But that summer Lizzie still played school with baby Lulu.